HOM

JEANNE WILLIS   PADDY DONNELLY

Andersen Press USA

For Owen, I hope you find a friend like Hom - P.D.

For David and Hermione Chambers - J.W.

American edition published in 2022 by Andersen Press USA,

an imprint of Andersen Press Ltd.

www.andersenpressusa.com

First published in Great Britain in 2021 by Andersen Press Ltd.,

20 Vauxhall Bridge Road, London SW1V 2SA

Distributed in the United States and Canada by

Lerner Publishing Group, Inc.

241 First Avenue North

Minneapolis, MN 55401 USA

For reading levels and more information, look up this title at www.lernerbooks.com.

Library of Congress Cataloging-in-Publication Data Available

ISBN 978-1-72844-971-5

2–TOPPAN–3/18/22

I've never told anyone about Hom.
No one knows he exists. Only me.
And you–because I trust you.

The grown-ups mustn't know about him.
They'll come and catch him and take him
away. But this is his home. He won't be
happy in their world. Hom is a peace-loving
creature. I don't know what kind
of a creature exactly.

It doesn't matter to me.
He's just Hom.

I met him after the shipwreck.
I swam to a deserted island,
far away.

Not one person came to
find me, but . . .

Hom did.

We'd never seen
anything like each
other. I'm not sure who
was more scared—me
or him! We laughed
about that later.

He's hairier than me,

but not as tall.

I don't know how old he is.
It's not important.

We're much more
alike than different.

Hom is the last of his kind. He had a family once.
There are drawings of them in his cave.

What happened to them?
He could not say.
But I know he misses
them beyond words.

I often think about my own
family. Did they survive
the shipwreck?
I hope so.

I've drawn them on the cave
wall next to Hom's.

I wrote them a message saying I'm safe.
I put it in a bottle and threw it out to sea.
Hom hugged me like he knew how I felt.

We've learned a lot
from each other. Hom
showed me which fruit is safe to eat.
Which is good, or I'd have starved.

There's no fresh water on the island.
I'd have died of thirst, but Hom fetched coconuts.
He cracked them open, and I drank the milk.

He gave me his favorite stone.
It was shaped like an ax
and felt strangely familiar, like
I'd held it a million years ago.

Hom is better at running than me.
He can run for days . . .
and nights.

I love it when we go hunting.

But it was me who taught him how to make fire.

Hom was thrilled when he saw his first flame. I'll never forget how his eyes lit up.

I gave him my toy car. He loved it. He'd never seen wheels before. He plays with it for hours.

Between us, we made a go-cart.

I fetched the driftwood, Hom did the chopping.
It was a bit wobbly but . . .

it worked!

We had so much fun, but then I saw a rescue ship.

My heart sank. It was my chance to go home, but . . .

I couldn't take Hom with me. And I couldn't bear to
leave him. If the sailors came ashore and saw him,
his life would never be the same. So . . .

... I hid with Hom until the sailors sailed away.

To this day, no one
knows I'm here.
Only you. But please
don't tell anyone
where I am . . .

or who I'm with. Hom is the only one of his kind. I must protect him.

I was the first person to see him and I promised him that I will be the last. Help me keep my promise until I come home.

Then you can tell the whole world about Hom.
And when people ask what kind of creature he was,
you can put your hand on your heart and say . . .

. . . he was peace-loving, happy, and free.